happy 2nd birthday
Lochlan !
love from auntie Jiel xo

GookShiGgoRengEe Village

"GookShiGgoRengEe Village" is a place where the stories of our past's children are still alive.

The children's work, play, and customs are alive with vivid traces of their laughter and tears.

They appear small and insignificant in comparison to the large extravagant culture

at the center of all the attention, therefore the village has gathered such looked-over,

gap-filling odds and ends of our culture.

Today, our children go back and forth from school to other varieties of extra-curricular institutes,

holding hamburgers in their hands, and they play with computers and televisions.

GookShiGgoRengEe

- is a dialect of the GyeongSangBukDo Region
  in South Korea
- is a dialectal term for GookSooGgoRee
- means the 'cut ends of the noodle dough'

There were days when children would freely run around through the mountains and fields, eating and playing with the flowers and the grass they would pick up along the way.

Their imagination did not cease to grow as they played in the evening under the moonlight by stepping on the shadows that the moon provided for them, and by counting the stars in the sky.

Heaven and earth were all in the possession of our children.

Unfortunately, the abundant life and nature that our children have been blessed with for thousands of years is now almost disappearing and being forgotten.

GookShiGgoRengEe Village would like to become a stepping stone to connect the children of today with the past by restoring the variety of our lost and niched culture.

GookShiGgoRengEe Village 1

Poo Cake

Text © Lee, Choon hee 2003
Illustrations © Park, Ji hoon 2003

The first Korean edition was published by e*public Co., Ltd. in 2003.
This English edition was published by e*public Co., Ltd. in 2008.

ISBN 978-89-6224-178-5 | 978-89-6224-535-6(set)

Poo Cake

Written by Lee, Choon hee

Illustrated by Park, Ji hoon

safari

"Puuuuushhh!

   Poopoo, you slow poopoo!

   Hurry, come out quickly!"

Joon ho sang as he shook his behind

sitting over the toilet.

Slip~ Splash!
Joon ho slipped and fell
into the big bucket
full of all different shapes
and colors of poopoo.
The poopoo was gold, black,
hard, soft, and watery...!
As he waved his arms
to get out of the bucket,
he screamed
"Mommy! Mommy!"

"Joon ho!"

Mom was surprised and came running to the toilet.

"Woof, woof, woof!"

The puppy ran alongside mom.

"Boohoo~"

"Oh, honey, it's alright. Mommy is here now," mom said

as she pulled him out of the bucket full of poopoo.

"Boohoo~"

"It's okay, it's okay. I will wash you clean,"

mom said as she took off his dirty clothes.

"What kind of poo smell is this?"

Grandma frowned and complained

as she walked into the yard on her way back from the neighborhood.

"Tut, tut. You should have been more careful, Joon ho.

 Don't you know that you may die early if you fall into

 the toilet bucket?"

"What?" Both Joon ho and mom cried out.

Grandma then smiled at mom and whispered something into her ear.

Mom ran quickly into the kitchen.

After she had washed some rice, she crushed it into

fine powder and then mixed it with water and salt.

She also boiled red beans to put inside the rice dough.

Grandma sat down on the floor and began to make rice cake.

"Grandma, what kind of rice cake is this?"

"This is poo cake! It's for the child who's fallen into the toilet bucket."

"Haha!"

Joon ho burst out into laughter as he heard the word 'POO CAKE'.

"This cake can save the life of the child by driving away the evil spirits," grandma said.

Then, she continued to make poo cake with all her heart.

Mom put the poo cake in
a huge pot and lit the fireplace.
Crack, pop, crack!
The dry firewood began to burn.
When mom saw the steam
rising out of the pot,
she opened the lid.
"Wow! That looks delicious!
 Can I have a piece right now?"
"Hold on for a minute, dear.
 We need to give it to the toilet
 ghost first."
"The toilet ghost?"

"Yes, she's the mean ghost bride living in the toilet," explained grandma, "she played tricks to make you fall into the toilet bucket. If we don't please her, we will get into bigger trouble."

"Really?"

Joon ho's eyes widened in horror.

"But don't worry, honey. The toilet ghost loves poo cake and it should make her happy!"

Grandma put a plate of poo cake in front of the toilet

and prayed to the toilet ghost.

"Toilet ghost, toilet ghost!

  Please eat this delicious poo cake

  and don't be angry anymore."

Joon ho bowed with grandma and mom.

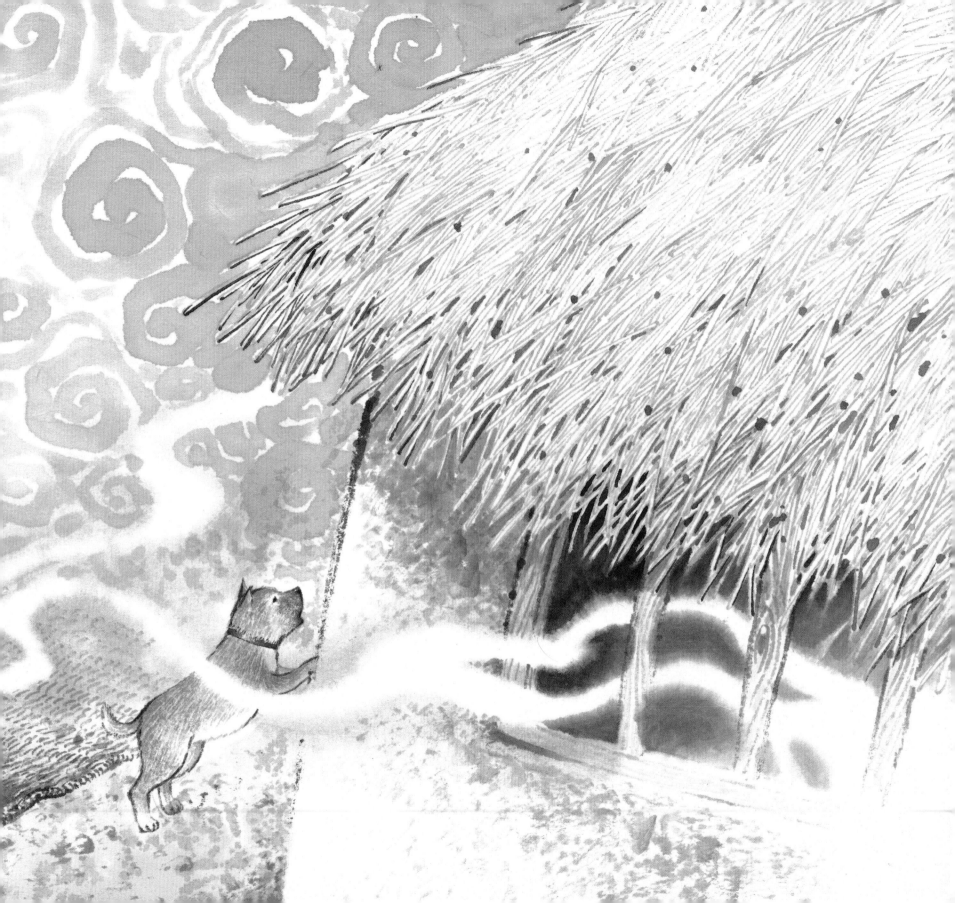

"Uggghhhh!"

The toilet ghost suddenly popped out of the toilet

fluttering her long hair and gasped,

"Hee hee hee~ I love poo cake. Let me have a bite!"

"Oh yes, toilet ghost! Please eat this delicious poo cake
 and allow this child to live a long life."
Grandma and mom prayed more eagerly.

"Toilet... ghost... now that you ate the poo cake please spare my life..."
Joon ho stuttered as his voice shook with fear.
"Yum yum~ This is the best poo cake I have ever tasted! Hee hee hee!"
The toilet ghost disappeared and laughed noisily.

When the toilet ghost was gone,

grandma put the poo cake into Joon ho's mouth.

"One, two, three... and seven."

After Joon ho ate as many pieces of poo cake as he

was years old, mom filled a basket with the poo cake.

"Joon ho, walk around the neighborhood

and give out this poo cake."

"Why, mom?"

"Because it brings good luck when we share the poo cake with others

    after we've said our prayers to the ghost.

    Oh, and don't forget to shout 'poo cake, poo cake' as you do that."

"Awww, that's embarrassing!"

"Poo cake! Poo cake!" shouted Joon ho loudly.

"Woof, woof, woof!" the puppy ran alongside Joon ho.

The neighbors greeted Joon ho.

"Oh, you brought the lucky cake!"